Here Comes Peter Cottontail

Illustrated by
Patrick T. McRae

Ideals Publishing Corp.
Nashville, Tennessee

PETER COTTONTAIL by Steve Nelson and Jack Rollins
Copyright © 1950 by Hill and Range Songs, Inc.
Copyright renewed, Assigned to Chappell & Co., Inc.
(Intersong Music, Publisher)

Illustrations © 1985 by Ideals Publishing Corporation
Published by Ideals Publishing Corporation,
Nelson Place at Elm Hill Pike, Nashville, TN 37214.
All rights reserved. Printed and bound in U.S.A.
Published simultaneously in Canada.

ISBN 0-8249-8106-5

Here comes Peter Cottontail,
Hoppin' down the bunny trail,
Hippity hoppin', Easter's on its way.

Bringin' every girl and boy

As we all got out our history textbooks, Lindsey turned around to whisper to me. "Here!" she said, handing me one of her colorful wallets. "Now you'll have something to put the money in before you send it."

Help in Times of Need

Following Hurricane Katrina, more than 90 countries offered to help the people of New Orleans. Bangladesh pledged $1 million. Thailand offered to send 60 doctors and nurses to help the injured and sick. Kuwait, Qatar, and the United Arab Emirates sent large donations, while Germany sent high-speed pumps to help reduce the amount of floodwater in the city. The Netherlands sent experts on levee construction.

Look, Look Again

This photo shows New Orleans residents being rescued by military helicopter in the aftermath of Hurricane Katrina. Use the photo to answer the questions below:

1. How would someone who had waited days for rescue after Hurricane Katrina react to this photo? Why?

2. How would a rescue worker describe this photo to a friend?

3. What questions might someone who hadn't experienced Hurricane Katrina firsthand have about this photo?

Baskets full of Easter joy,

Things to make your Easter bright and gay.

He's got jelly beans for Tommy,

Colored eggs for sister Sue,

There's an orchid for your Mommy

And an Easter bonnet, too.

Oh! here comes Peter Cottontail,
Hoppin' down the bunny trail,
Hippity hoppity, Happy Easter day.

Here comes Peter Cottontail,
Hoppin' down the bunny trail,

Look at him stop, and listen to him say:
"Try to do the things you should."

Maybe if you're extra good,

He'll roll lots of Easter eggs your way.

You'll wake up on Easter morning
And you'll know that he was there

When you find those choc'late bunnies
That he's hiding ev'rywhere.

Oh! here comes Peter Cottontail,
Hoppin' down the bunny trail,

Hippity hoppity, Happy Easter day.